Aliens for Lunch

By Jonathan Etra
and Stephanie Spinner

Illustrated by Steve Björkman

A STEPPING STONE BOOK

Random House New York

Library of Congress Cataloging-in-Publication Data:
Etra, Jonathan. Aliens for lunch / by Jonathan Etra and Stephanie Spinner ; illustrated by Steve Björkman. p. cm. "A Stepping stone book." SUMMARY: When their bag of microwave popcorn explodes and a space alien emerges, Richard and Henry join him on a top-secret interstellar mission to save the desserts of the universe. ISBN: 0-679-81056-0 (pbk.); 0-679-91056-5 (lib. bdg.) [1. Etraterrestrial beings—Fiction. 2. Science fiction.] I. Spinner, Stephanie. II. Björkman, Steve, ill. III. Title. PZ7.E854Ap 1991 [Fic]—dc20 90-39417

Manufactured in the United States of America 1 2 3 4 5 6 7 8 9 0

To Mom—J.E.
To Jane and Judy—S.S.

1.

"I should be happy," said Richard Bicker-staff. "But I'm not." He sighed loudly.

Henry Bell, Richard's best friend, grunted. He was lying on the floor next to Richard, reading a *Star Trek* comic. Henry was a boy of few words. Especially when he was reading.

"Want to know why?" asked Richard.

"You're hungry?" asked Henry without looking up. Richard was thin but he liked to eat. Strange junk food and gooey desserts were his favorites.

"No," said Richard. "It's worse than that."

"You spent your whole allowance and it's only Tuesday?"

This was true but Richard would not admit it. "Nope," he said. "It's because we are practically the only two people in the world who are stuck at home. Everyone—and I mean everyone—has gone away for Easter vacation. Except us." He sighed again.

Henry finally looked up. "Even Celia Drummond?" he asked. Celia was the tallest—and the prettiest—girl in their class.

"Disneyland," said Richard. "Jennifer is at Ocean World. Leroy is at the Baseball Hall of Fame. And George went to Tortola. I don't even know where that is!"

"Neither does George," said Henry. He turned back to his comic.

Just then Mrs. Bickerstaff appeared in the doorway. "I'm off to court," she said. Mrs. Bickerstaff was a lawyer. "I left some lunch for you guys. It's in the fridge. There's microwave popcorn, too—a free sample came in the mail today. You might like it. It's pepperoni flavor." She smiled. "If I'm not back in time for dinner, you can order a pizza. Have fun."

"Thanks, Mom," said Richard. As soon as he heard the front door close, he jumped up. "Popcorn!" he yelled. "Let's eat!"

The two friends ran to the kitchen. Henry opened the refrigerator and found a plate of sandwiches and some celery sticks. "Wow, great, celery," he said, taking a handful. "And look at these—avocado and sprout! Want one?" He took a bite out of a sandwich, then offered the plate to Richard. Lately Henry had begun eating healthy food. He liked green vegetables best. He ate bean sprouts, celery, cucumbers, broccoli, and zucchini every chance he got. It was the one thing about him that Richard thought was weird.

"No, thanks," said Richard, who hated vegetables. "I think I'll try the popcorn." He picked up a silver bag that was sitting on the counter. "Radical! It really *is* pepperoni flavor. And it's got a hologram of a spaceship on it."

"Kaboom Korn," read Henry, who was chewing noisily on a celery stick. "Sounds good." They read the directions on the package, set the oven, and put the popcorn in. There was a series of dull pops, like a drum-roll. The bag doubled in size. Then everything was quiet.

"Is it done?" asked Richard. Before Henry could say anything, there was a small boom. The bag suddenly blew up to the size of a watermelon and burst apart. The door of the oven banged open. Popcorn flew all over the kitchen. "Take cover!" yelled Richard. He threw himself under the table.

"Do not bother," said a loud voice. The pile of popcorn shifted. A small pink creature the color of bubblegum emerged.

"Aric!" cried Richard. Aric was a tiny alien from the planet Ganoob. He was also commander of the Interspace Brigade, warriors who fought trouble all over the galaxy. Many months ago he and Richard had saved Earth from a deadly invasion of space creatures. Then he had gone back to his home planet. Richard had really missed him.

"Wow! It's great to see you!" Richard turned to Henry. "It's Aric!" he said. "The alien I told you about! Remember?"

Henry stood there, his mouth open and his eyes glued to Aric. "Hi," he managed to say.

"I thought you only came to Earth freeze-dried in cereal," Richard said to Aric.

"Microwave beaming is the latest in budget transport methods," said Aric. "Much cheaper than freeze-drying. We save fifty thousand daktils—that's $18.04 in Earth money—each trip." He jumped down onto the kitchen counter. "But there is no time to chat. The universe calls. Are you ready?"

"Sure!" cried Richard happily. "What are we going to do? Fight off another invasion? The new gym teacher looks like an alien to me."

Henry laughed. Richard could tell he was really excited.

"Not this time," said Aric. "The new mission is easier, but just as important. One of our cargo ships has gone astray. It was bound for the planet Threll, but now it is heading in the direction of Grax. The Graxians are big bullies who are always getting into trouble. We fear they have hijacked the ship. I must capture it and put it back on course for Threll. Will you help?"

"Sure!" said Henry.

"How come the ship was hijacked?" asked Richard.

Aric's little pink face turned serious. "You must swear to reveal nothing," he said. "This mission is top-secret. The very peace of the cosmos is at stake."

"I swear," said Richard. "Really."

"Me too," said Henry.

Aric sat down cross-legged on a potholder. "The ship is carrying something very important," he said. "Something rare, precious, and vital to cosmic harmony."

"What is it?" both boys asked.

"XTC-1000. The dessert element."

2.

"The dessert element?" asked Richard.

"Yes. The vital ingredient that makes all dessert taste good. You have no idea how important it is. No XTC-1000, no dessert. No dessert, no peace." Aric sighed. "We have never had a serious problem before. We have always shipped on time—every 11,976 years."

"Twelve thousand years till dessert?" Richard gasped.

"11,976," corrected Aric. "That's how long the XTC-1000 keeps working—if a planet runs out, dessert still looks the same, but it tastes terrible."

"So then how come the Graxians hijacked your ship?" asked Richard. "Didn't they have enough XTC?"

"They got the correct shipment for a planet of their size a mere three thousand years ago," said Aric. "Enough XTC-1000 for eons. All they had to do was leave it alone so that it could enter their atmosphere properly—automatically, over time. But did they do it? No! They were greedy pigs! They ignored the directions. They deliberately tampered with the container. The XTC-1000 was released all at once and the Graxians went crazy. There were years and years of wild parties and disgusting food fights. And now, of course, it is all gone. There hasn't been a decent cookie on the planet since King Boobrik the Heavy. So they are desperate."

"I'll bet," said Henry.

"Life without dessert is a terrible thing," said Aric. "I hope you don't have to find that out for yourselves . . ." His voice trailed off.

The boys stared at him. "What do you mean?" asked Richard, who thought there was no point in eating unless you got dessert.

"Never mind. Never mind," boomed Aric in

his loud voice. "Just gather your weapons."

"Weapons?" asked Richard.

"Of course. Ion wave guns. Vortex beams. Laser cannons."

"Great. Where are they?"

"You do not have them?"

"No."

Aric looked worried. "They were sent hours ago," he said. "Right after we got the news about the hijacking. We used a new method— holo-faxing. Only ten thousand daktils, or three and a half Earth dollars per item. Very cheap. The budget committee swore it would work. Are you sure they are not around here somewhere? Under the magazines? In the bathtub?"

Richard was sure he hadn't seen any weapons. "Nope," he said. "Sorry."

"Well, we will have to find *something,*" said Aric. "Open that," he ordered, pointing to a kitchen drawer. Richard pulled it open. Aric jumped in. He began hauling things out. A cheese grater. A wooden spoon. A tea strainer. A potato peeler.

Richard began to help him. "What exactly are we looking for?" he asked.

"Graxians are bullies. Cowards, too. Do you have anything that makes noise? Anything that might startle them?"

"What about this?" asked Henry. He held up a cordless electric eggbeater. When he turned it on, it made a loud whiny sound.

"Not bad," said Aric.

"How about this?" Richard held up a spray can of soy sauce. "Mom uses it on her sushi. It's kind of scary." He waved the can in the air. It rattled loudly. "It's sticky, too," he added. "And it smells."

For a moment Aric looked a little uncertain. "I wish I could remember what the Brigade manual said about fighting Graxians," he said, half to himself.

All of a sudden Richard felt very nervous. What were he and Henry getting into? Should they really try to fight aliens with kitchen gadgets? But Henry didn't seem worried. And Aric kept barking orders.

"Now prepare yourselves. Deep space is very cold, but we will not be in it long." He jumped onto Richard's shoulder. "Hold hands!" he cried. "Close your eyes! Have your weapons ready!"

Richard stuck the spray can into his pocket. Henry wedged the eggbeater into his waistband. Richard took Henry's hand with his eyes closed.

"To battle!" cried Aric. There was a flash of yellow light. Richard's stomach felt as if it were dropping out. And he was cold, too—so cold it was almost like burning. His ears hurt. Then he heard a familiar voice. "Prepare to attack!" ordered Aric.

3.

Richard opened his eyes. He and Henry were sitting on the floor of a giant white room. One whole wall was made of dials and screens. The room was empty.

"Where are we?" Richard asked.

"This is the control room of the space-craft," Aric said. "And we are in luck. The Graxians must be in another part of the ship. We may not have to fight them."

He leaped to the control panel and began pressing buttons and turning knobs. "In just another moment I can put the ship on course for Threll," he told the boys. "Then the Threllians will get their XTC-1000. Conflict will be avoided. The Interspace Brigade thanks you for your support. As soon as funds are available, you will each receive a special Ganoobian T-shirt. When you wear it females will be unable to resist you."

"Ugh!" said Henry.

"Great!" said Richard.

Aric kept working at the controls.

Suddenly the ship slowed almost to a stop. "By the Great Kazook!" muttered Aric. "What gives?" Then a section of one wall slid open. A very big orange creature with fins on its head and sharp shiny claws walked in. Behind him were six more creatures. They were all bristling with weapons. Richard's heart raced. He had a horrible feeling he knew what they were—Graxians!

He was right.

"Disarm them," said the leader. "Welcome to Grax," he added smoothly. "Count Wali Dood at your service."

"Stop right there!" said Aric. "In the name of the Interspace Brigade, I arrest you! Quick, Henry, the eggbeater!"

Henry turned on the eggbeater and pointed it at the guards. Richard pulled the spray can out of his pocket and rattled it menacingly in the air. The guards started laughing. Then they simply took the eggbeater and the spray can away.

Richard felt like a total jerk.

Wali Dood snickered. "I truly enjoy the Ganoobian sense of humor," he told Aric. "You know, we have a best-selling book on Grax. It's called *Ganoob, You Make Me Laugh*. Some

day soon, when you are pining away in one of our small, smelly jail cells, you really should read it."

"It is you who will pine away—in a clean, well-lit Ganoobian jail!" shouted Aric. "Now put your weapons down and be quiet!"

Wali Dood chuckled again. "Allow me to explain," he said. "This ship is under our control. All systems have been disconnected. We will shortly be landing on Grax. There the ship will be stripped of its cargo. The XTC-1000 will be ours. And there is nothing you or your pathetic Space Brigade can do about it."

Richard and Henry looked at each other. "Whoa," said Richard quietly to his friend.

"No!" shouted Aric. "The cargo *must* go to Threll! The Threllians are quick to anger. If they do not get their XTC-1000 on time they will become dangerous. They will attack the nearest planet with a plentiful dessert supply." He turned to the boys. "I am afraid that means Earth," he said.

4.

Minutes later Richard and Henry were herded off the ship. Richard had always wanted to go to another planet, but now that he was on one, he didn't like it much. Grax was ugly. The sky was brown and the landscape was flat and muddy. It reminded Richard of an empty lot after a rainstorm. Then there were the Graxians. Not only did they smell funny—like his mother's nail polish remover—but they were rough and mean. They pushed Henry and Richard with their big orange paws and threatened to hit Richard when he stumbled.

That was scary—their claws looked really sharp.

The guards took them into a big gray building that reminded Richard of a castle. Then they shoved them down one long cold gray hallway after another, even though the boys walked as fast as they could. Richard didn't dare say anything to Henry, who was walking ahead of him. And he couldn't figure out what was going on with Aric. As soon as they were off the ship, the little alien had crawled inside Richard's shirt pocket. Richard could hear him muttering to himself about weapons and manuals in a confused way.

"I thought Graxians were cowards!" Richard whispered to him. There was no answer.

Being a prisoner on a strange gray smelly planet full of hulking bullies was not a great way to spend Easter vacation, thought Richard. He was scared.

He was even more scared when they were led before King Boobrik the Heavy. Boobrik was much bigger than Wali Dood. And he looked even meaner—like a rhino in a bad mood, only orange. When the boys were led up to his throne, he stared at them with tiny black eyes that were set very close together in his big leathery face.

"Earthlings!" he sneered. "You are even smaller than I thought. Perhaps I will have you encased in plastic and hung from a key chain." He turned to the count. "How strange that their puny planet has such tasty desserts," he snarled. "Now, where is it?"

"Here, Majesty," said the count. He handed

Boobrik a small square package tied with string. Written on the package in big letters were the words PURE XTC-1000. ANOTHER FINE PRODUCT OF GANOOB. THIS END UP. STORE IN A COOL, DRY PLACE FOR 11,976 YEARS. DO NOT BREAK SAFETY SEAL. BEWARE OF IMITATIONS.

Boobrik grunted. The fins on his head shook with excitement. "Tonight," he said, "when the sky darkens to a deep, rich brown and the air is warm, I will do it. I will release the XTC! All of it!"

The count smiled. "Praise be to the Heavy!" he cried. "Praise be!" and "Heavy!" shouted some of the guards.

Richard felt he had to say something. "But—what about Threll?" he asked. "If they don't get their XTC, won't they attack Earth?"

Boobrik chuckled. So did the guards. "Probably," said the king. "And you miserable Earthlings can watch it happen. We get excellent reception on our Earth Channel. It will be amusing to see them strip your planet of all its desserts." He turned to the count. "Make sure there's a video screen in their cell," he said.

Richard felt something on his shoulder. It was Aric.

"Boobrik!" cried the tiny alien. "Stop this madness. Free us. Let us make our delivery to Threll before it is too late!"

Boobrik frowned. "Ganoobians are such pests," he snarled. "Take him away and freeze him."

"No!" gasped Richard. But two guards yanked Aric from Richard's shoulder and lumbered out of the throne room.

"This is bad," said Richard.

"It's not that bad," said Henry. "At least we have TV." The boys had been put in a room with two beds, a desk, and a video screen. Henry had turned it on and found *Star Trek*. It was in some strange alien language, but that didn't matter to Henry. "Look!" he said. "Mr. Spock is laughing. I've never seen this episode."

"I don't believe you're watching *Star Trek* at a time like this," said Richard. "The Graxians could burst in here any second and do something horrible to us. How can you be so calm?"

"You were the one who wanted to get away for vacation," said Henry.

"Not this far," Richard said. "Besides, I'm really worried about Aric. We've got to save him and get out of here. This whole situation is totally out of control. Don't you care?"

"Sure I care," said Henry. "I just don't know what to do about it. Do you?"

Richard sighed. He didn't have a clue. "How about changing the channel?" he said.

But changing the channel only made things worse. When Henry turned the dial he got the Earth Channel—and some bad news.

"I am standing outside Dunkin' Donuts headquarters in Randolph, Massachusetts," a news reporter was saying. "Here, only a few hours ago, security guards claimed they saw an unidentified flying object hanging in the sky. And this is only one of a rash of sightings that were reported last night. We've had similar reports from a Carvel ice cream shop in Queens, New York, from the nation's largest chocolate factory in Hershey, Pennsylvania, and from Gummi Bear headquarters in New Brunswick, New Jersey. What do you make of it, Jim?"

The camera went to a newscaster sitting at a desk. "It's too soon to tell, Derek," he said. "But the government states that there is absolutely no cause for alarm. An investigation is under way." He smiled. "And now let's hear from our weatherperson—"

Richard and Henry looked at each other. "Those must be the Threllians! They're getting ready to invade!" Richard said. Henry turned off the set. He groaned. "I take back what I said before. This *is* bad. In fact, it's terrible."

Hearing Henry say this made Richard feel even worse. "Those guys on TV don't even understand what's happening," he said. "The Threllians could attack any minute. And then what? Earth without dessert will be a disaster."

"Maybe there won't be any Earth left," said Henry. "Maybe the Threllians will just wipe out the whole planet. And then we'll never get home."

"Gross!" yelped Richard, looking around the cell. Its walls were gray, and just as Wali Dood had said, it was small and smelly. Richard thought of his own room. Then he thought of his mom and tears sprang into his eyes.

Just then the door of the cell clanged open. Richard and Henry jumped to their feet as two guards walked in. "Get up!" said the first one.

"Don't try anything or we'll freeze you," said the second one. He shoved the boys out into a long gray hallway. "Now move it!" he ordered.

"Where are you taking us?" asked Richard. He was so scared he was sweating. "To some horrible torture chamber?" The guards didn't answer. They just grinned at each other. Then they led the boys all the way down the hall. Finally they came to a set of big gray metal doors, and the first guard snickered. "We don't need torture chambers here, Earth boy. We have prison dining halls. We're taking you to lunch."

5.

The prison dining hall was big, gray, noisy, and lined with rows of tables. It was a lot like the cafeteria in Richard's school.

"Sit down," said the first guard, pushing the boys onto a crowded bench. "Eat hearty," said the second guard, giving Richard one last shove before he walked off.

Richard sneaked a look around. Not all the prisoners at the table were Graxians. Next to Richard was a big blue creature who was mostly scales and teeth. It held out a claw that looked like it could slice a turkey in half in one stroke.

"I'm a Turinga death machine," it hissed into Richard's ear. "Please pass the bemush."

"Uh—what's bemush?" asked Richard. He looked up and down the table nervously.

The claw reached over Richard and grabbed a bowl of lumpy pink paste. "This," hissed the creature from Turinga. It poured the paste all over the food on its plate. Then it emptied the whole mess into a hole on top of its head. There was a long, loud flushing sound. Then the Turinga death machine snorted. "Even bemush can't make this stuff taste good," it said.

Richard inspected his own plate. It was

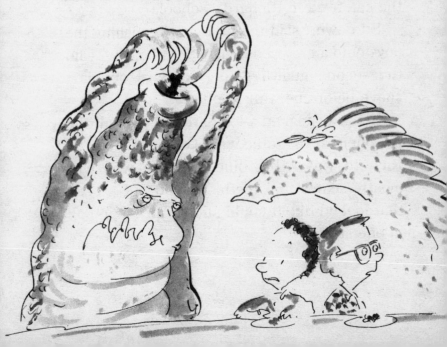

covered with a mixture of brownies, peanut brittle, and green and purple jellybeans. His spirits lifted just a little bit. They were all things he really liked. And, he realized, he was hungry. But when he popped some of the mixture into his mouth, he got a nasty shock. It tasted like an old spitball.

"Ugh," he said to Henry, who was sitting across from him. "No wonder the Graxians are desperate. Have you tasted your lunch?"

Before Henry could answer, the Graxian sitting next to him started pounding his claws on the table. "I can't eat this," he whined. "There's no whipped cream on it. We always get whipped cream when we have Earth desserts."

There were grunts of agreement from the other prisoners. A few of them pounded on the table, too.

A huge guard lurched over to the table. He was carrying a heavy metal canister. "Who wants whipped cream?" he asked.

"I do," said the Graxian next to Richard.

"Me too," said the Turinga death machine.

"Me too. Me too," said some of the other prisoners.

The guard brought the canister down, hard, onto the head of the big Graxian. He slid to the floor, unconscious. "There you are," sneered the guard. "We try to keep our prisoners happy. Anyone else?" He looked at Richard and Henry. "You want some whipped cream, too? Or a cherry, maybe?"

"No, sir," said Richard quickly.

"Me neither," said Henry. "But—"

"But what?"

"I wouldn't mind some vegetables if you have them."

The instant Henry spoke these words, deep silence fell over the hall. "Wh—what?" asked the guard, backing away slightly.

"Vegetables," said Henry. His voice sounded very loud in the stillness. "You know. Zucchini? Asparagus? Green pepper?" The guard backed away a little more.

"Or how about celery?" asked Henry. He pulled a little plastic bag out of his pants pocket. In it were the celery sticks Mrs. Bickerstaff had left for lunch. "Like these," said Henry. He held them up.

The guard's little eyes opened very wide, and he made a strange gagging sound. Then his eyes closed and he fell over in a heap.

"Give me some of those," Richard said to Henry. Hundreds of terrified eyes watched as Henry handed over a bunch of celery sticks. Hundreds of terrified Graxian bodies dropped to the floor as Richard waved the sticks in the air.

"These work a whole lot better than spray soy sauce," he said to Henry. "Now let's get out of here."

6.

Once they were outside the prison dining hall Richard and Henry realized their troubles were by no means over. They had absolutely no idea how to find Aric. Or how to escape once they did. They weren't sure how the celery worked on the Graxians, either. Did it make them faint for a long time? Or for only a few minutes?

On top of everything else, they were starving. "I could kick myself for not eating some of that popcorn Mom left us for lunch," said Richard. "Maybe we should look for the prison kitchen before we try to find Aric."

"But Graxian food is horrible," Henry reminded him. He took a bite out of a celery stick. "Too bad you don't like this stuff," he said.

"Henry!" shouted Richard. "Stop! You're eating our weapons!"

"Oops, sorry," said Henry. "I forgot." He put the celery back in his pocket. Then he thought for a moment. "You know," he said slowly, "maybe we really should try the kitchen. Not for food, but to find Aric. I mean, where would they freeze him, anyway? In a freezer, right?"

"You're a genius!" said Richard. "Let's go!"

Henry was pretty smart about finding the kitchen, too. He guessed that it was probably next to the dining hall, and he was right.

The boys tiptoed in. The kitchen was like most of the other Graxian rooms they had been in—big, cold, gray, and smelly. They started down the center, which was lined with rows of tall gray counters. Then they heard a sound—a voice—from the far end.

They ducked. "And it's looking stranger by the minute, Derek," said a man's voice.

"There've been six separate sightings in the last two hours alone."

The boys realized they were hearing another television newscast from Earth. But who was watching it? They crept through the rest of the kitchen as quietly as they could.

"Can you see a pattern in it, Jim?" asked another voice.

"It looks candy-related to me," Jim answered solemnly. Then his voice rose in surprise. "What do you know?" he exclaimed. "We've just gotten news of sightings over the Swiss Chocolate Institute and the Twinkie plant in Japan! Can this be happening all over the globe?"

By now Richard and Henry were close to the television—close enough to see two big leathery Graxian guards watching it. One was eating hot fudge sauce out of a bowl the size of a sink. As the boys tiptoed closer, he threw down his spoon.

"Who am I kidding?" he asked in disgust. "I can't eat this stuff. It tastes like esht." He turned off the television. "It's a good thing we got that new supply of XTC," he said. "I'm about ready to kill for a decent dessert."

The other guard laughed. "Sounds like the Thrells are, too. Boy, I'm glad we don't have to tangle with them. Those poor little Earthlings won't know what hit 'em. Be fun to watch on the tube," he added.

"Speaking of watching," said the first guard, "have you checked the Ganoobian yet?"

"He's in the freezer. What's there to check?"

"Those were Wali Dood's orders," said the first guard.

"Orders, shmorders," said the second guard, getting heavily to his feet. "They should pay us better for working so hard." He lumbered over to the far end of the kitchen and pulled a handle set into the wall. The freezer door swung open and great clouds of white drifted into the room. "Looks okay to me," he called. Then he made a gagging sound and toppled over. Henry had thrust the celery sticks right into his face.

Richard and Henry looked at each other and grinned. "I have new respect for vegetables," whispered Richard. "It's about time," said Henry. He reached over the guard's body into the freezer. There was Aric, sitting on a stack of frozen chocolate cakes. He was frozen, too—all scrunched up like a wad of gray chewed bubblegum.

"He looks awful," gasped Richard.

"Well, he's always getting beamed around the galaxy in cereal boxes and popcorn. Being frozen shouldn't bother him too much. I bet he'll be okay."

Richard hoped Henry was right. He picked Aric up and put him inside his shirt so he'd warm up faster. "Eeyow!" he yelped. It was like trying to cuddle an ice ball.

"Hey, Sherbrik! What's going on over there?" shouted the first guard. He poked his head

around a counter and saw Richard and Henry standing over Sherbrik's body.

Richard thought fast. "Just show him a tiny bit of the celery," he whispered to Henry. "Or else he'll faint before we can find out how to get out of here."

"Good thinking," said Henry.

"Hold it. Don't move," growled the guard. But before he could say anything else, Henry was holding the celery up at him so that only about a half-inch showed. The guard stopped in his tracks and swallowed hard. Then he turned from orange to yellow.

"How do we get to the palace?" demanded Richard. "Tell us!"

"Put that thing away, please," whimpered the guard. "I can't stand it. It's making me sick." The fins on his head wobbled and he started to sway.

"Where's the palace?" asked Henry. "Quick—or I'll show you the whole thing." He held the celery a little closer.

"Aargh! Through the kitchen, up the stairs to level seven. Take the first door on your right, go down the passageway, and you're practically in the throne room. Now will you put it away?" the guard whined.

"That's it? You're not leaving anything out?"

"No. I swear. Sometimes the wamu prowls around outside the throne room looking for crawling things to eat, but . . ."

"What's a wamu?" asked Richard suspiciously.

"A lizard. Boobrik keeps it as a pet. He says it's harmless."

"Thanks," said Richard.

"You'd better sit down on the floor," Henry told the guard. As soon as he was sitting, Henry waved the celery stick—the whole thing—at him. "Sorry," he said as the guard toppled over in a faint. He turned to Richard. "We'd better hurry," he said.

So they did. They raced through the kitchen to the stairs and up each flight as fast as they could go. There was a window on the sixth-level landing, showing a brown sky that was turning darker at the edges. Down below in a large courtyard a crowd of Graxians stood silently.

"What are they doing down there?" panted Henry.

"They're waiting," Richard panted back.

"For Boobrik to release the XTC."

"Geez. I hope we're not too late to stop him."

"Don't say that," said Richard. "Don't even think it."

They sprinted up the last flight and burst through the door on their right. The second the door closed behind them they heard a loud, angry hiss. And then a giant green lizard sprang at them.

Henry froze. Richard's knees buckled and his eyes clamped shut. The next thing he knew, he was on the floor and a warm forked tongue was licking his forehead. He forced himself to open his eyes. A great big scaly lizard face was staring down at him. Its yellow eyes blinked slowly.

"I think it likes you," said Henry, who was standing as far away as he could get.

Richard looked up. It sure seemed that way. If a giant lizard could look friendly, this was the way it would look. Almost as if it were smiling. The wamu began gently nuzzling Richard's side.

"Oh, no!" Henry shouted. "It's got its nose in your pants pocket! It's after the celery!"

Richard slid away from the wamu—too late. The big lizard was busy chewing. A few pale-green strings hung from its mouth. It swished its tail.

"Great!" Richard moaned. "How many sticks do we have left?"

Henry reached into his pocket. "Two," he said.

"Let's hope that's enough to overpower thousands of Graxians," said Richard. He stood up. A soggy wet lump rolled down his chest and started kicking him.

"Where am I? Let me out of here!" came a familiar voice from underneath Richard's shirt.

Aric had finally thawed.

7.

Richard pulled the little alien out of his shirt. Aric was still cold, but at least he was bright pink again. He got to his feet, standing on Richard's hand.

"Aric—how are you?" asked Richard.

"Fine, fine," said Aric gruffly. He shivered and looked around. When he saw the wamu he flinched. "By the Great Kazook!" he exclaimed. "What's that?"

"Boobrik's pet wamu," said Richard. "Don't worry. It's friendly." The wamu looked at Aric, its yellow eyes large. Suddenly its tongue flicked out. Aric took a quick step backward.

"Down, wamu!" said Henry. The lizard stood still, but its eyes stayed on Aric. "We'd better get out of here," Henry said to Richard. "I think it thinks Aric is food. Remember how the guard said it feeds on little crawling things?"

"Have some respect!" barked Aric. "You are

referring to the commander of the Interspace Brigade, not an insect!"

"I don't think it can tell the difference," said Richard.

"Anyway, we really should get going," said Henry.

"Going? Going where?" asked Aric.

"To get the XTC," said Richard. "Don't you remember?"

"I'm not sure," said the alien. "I feel a little fuzzy."

Richard and Henry exchanged worried looks. "Aric," said Richard, "we're on Grax. We're prisoners. Boobrik is probably looking for us right now. And he'll probably do something horrible to us when he finds us."

"Boobrik!" Suddenly Aric looked a little more alert. "That slimeball froze me, didn't he?"

The boys nodded yes.

"No wonder I cannot think straight," said Aric. "My memory always goes when I am frozen. I will be fine in a few minutes."

"We don't have a few minutes. We're in kind of a hurry," said Henry.

"That's the understatement of the century," said Richard.

"Okay. All right." Aric's eyes closed as if he was thinking very hard. At last he spoke. "I will make us invisible," he said. "That way we can get to Boobrik without being seen. And it will be easy for us to escape with the XTC-1000."

"Great idea!" said Richard.

"Thank you," said Aric, looking pleased with himself.

"Hey!" said Henry. "How come you didn't do this before?"

"It is very expensive," said Aric. "It is used only as a last resort."

"You mean you risked our lives to save a few measly dollars?" Henry looked shocked.

"The Brigade works on a very tight budget, young man," said Aric sternly. "Every ten minutes of vanishing costs half a million daktils—that is $183.15 in your money. Unvanishing costs a lot too—$86.40. Remember that the Brigade is responsible for forty-seven million worlds. If we were not careful we would be broke in a week."

"And I thought my dad was cheap," Henry muttered.

"Can we please get started?" begged Richard. "We really don't have time to stand around arguing."

"You are right," said Aric. "Put me in your shirt pocket," he told Richard. "Stay alert and stay together. Remember we will not be able to see one another. Or ourselves. And we will be invisible for only ten minutes. So speed is important. Listen for me in the throne room. I will be sending you my thoughts."

Richard and Henry got ready. Once they were holding hands Aric made a low humming sound that seemed to fill their heads. Richard and Henry found themselves humming, too. Then, as the wamu watched them with its bright yellow eyes, they all faded away into thin air. *?*

8.

When Richard saw the inside of the throne room, he was really glad he was invisible. It was packed. Hundreds and hundreds of big Graxians were standing at attention, their eyes locked on the platform at the end of the room. It was piled high with a feast of desserts. There were cakes, cookies, tubs of chocolate pudding, heaps of candy bars, and other things Richard didn't recognize. As they stared at it, many Graxians were drooling. It was not a pretty sight.

"Prepare yourselves!" Aric's voice sounded

very loud as it boomed inside Richard's head. "We must move up to the platform now."

Richard started pushing his way through the crowd. It wasn't easy. The Graxians didn't want to move, so he had to lean against them as hard as he could. And he had to do it holding Henry's hand. After a few minutes Richard was sweating and panting. So was Henry—Richard could feel his hand getting damp.

To make things even harder, the Graxians didn't like being pushed. So some of them started snarling and shoving at each other as the boys passed. But they got very quiet the moment Boobrik walked out onto the platform. Count Wali Dood followed, carrying a square package tied with string. Richard's heartbeat quickened when he saw it. The Graxians got excited, too. When Boobrik took the package from the count, the crowd sighed, drooled, and moved forward slightly.

"My fellow Graxians—" Boobrik began.

"Hurry!" Aric's voice was tense. "If he makes a short speech, we are sunk."

Why did Graxians have to be so big and

solid? wondered Richard. It was like squeezing through a room full of giant furniture. Giant, smelly, unfriendly furniture. He and Henry pushed a little harder.

"This is a glorious day in the history of our planet," Boobrik went on. "For when I release this precious element into the air, the Age of Woe will come to an end." He held up the package so that everyone could see it. "Will cupcakes taste like sponges anymore?" he cried. "No! They will finally taste like cupcakes again. And will jellybeans still taste like erasers?"

"No!" shouted a few Graxians.

"What'll they taste like?" screamed Boobrik.

There was a puzzled silence.

"Buttons?" suggested someone.

"No, no, no!" Boobrik raged. "They'll taste like jellybeans, you fools!" He waved the package above his head. "Jellybeans!" The crowd surged forward in a frenzy. Richard and Henry were carried along. Suddenly they found themselves exactly where they wanted to be—right at the edge of the platform.

"Get the XTC-1000, boys," came Aric's voice. Richard grabbed it.

Boobrik stood there with his mouth hanging open as the XTC left his claws and seemed to hang in the air.

"Let's go!" said Richard, wishing he could see Henry. Then, suddenly, he could. At first he was so surprised that he just stood there holding the package. But he recovered fast. He had to—Graxians were coming at him from all sides. And they all wanted one thing—to get that package away from him.

"Celery!" he shouted to Henry. Luckily Henry was faster than the Graxians. He whipped the celery out of his pocket and held it high above his head.

For an instant nothing happened. Then there was one very loud, shocked gasp from all the creatures in the throne room, and hundreds of large rushing bodies thudded to a dead halt.

Boobrik turned bright yellow at the sight of the celery. He screamed very loudly and lurched toward Henry. Richard's heart thumped. Boobrik was dangerously close to

Henry. But Henry, looking very pale, stood his ground. He even managed to wave the celery in Boobrik's face.

At this, Boobrik fell. And almost as if it were a signal, all the other Graxians fell, too.

"Awesome," said Richard, his voice shaking. And then they ran.

"Celery! I still cannot believe it!" Aric exclaimed. "I never knew it had such power over the Graxians. This information must go into the Brigade manual." He was sitting at the control panel of the cargo ship with Richard and Henry. The package of XTC-1000 was safely in Richard's lap, and they were only

minutes away from Threll. It looked as if their mission was finally a success. Aric had gotten them to the ship and then blasted off into space in record time. He had even gotten through to Threll with the message that dessert was on the way. But he was not really happy.

"How could I have made such a terrible mistake about the weapons?" he said. "If it had not been for you, the Interspace Brigade would be in disgrace. And of course Earth would be in ruins." His face was deep pink with embarrassment. "I owe the two of you a great deal."

"Oh, that's okay," said Richard. He hated to see Aric feeling bad. "We had a really good time. I'll never forget how Boobrik screamed when Henry flashed the celery at him. Or how Wali Dood's eyes kind of rolled around before he passed out. And the way all those crazed Graxians just . . . fell. It was great. Right, Henry?"

"Really," said Henry. "Besides, after this Richard won't laugh at me every time I say I like vegetables."

Suddenly the lights on the control panel started blinking. "We're coming into Threll's orbit," said Aric. "Hold tight for landing. And keep your fingers crossed. Threllians get very angry when they are kept waiting. And dessert is definitely late."

9.

But the Threllians weren't angry. They were overjoyed. Once they had their XTC, they couldn't do enough for Aric and the boys. Of course, they called off the invasion of Earth immediately. Then they threw a huge party for them called the Festival of 1,000 Desserts. They flew them to Thrillia, an entire continent of theme parks, rides, and video games, and gave them unlimited free tickets.

Best of all, they took them to the zoo. Unlike any other zoo in the universe, the Threllian Zoo contained extinct animals from many other worlds, including Earth. So Richard and Henry got to see live dinosaurs and even got to ride on them. Richard rode a brontosaurus that was as friendly as the wamu. Henry rode a triceratops that was much nicer looking than Boobrik.

Then, they all realized, it was time to go home. Aric was eager to get back to the Brigade. Henry didn't want to miss *Star Trek*. And Richard started to wonder about his mom.

"Do you think she's back yet?" he asked Aric. "I wouldn't want her to worry about me."

"No problem," Aric told him. "We've only been gone a few hours in Earth time. She won't even know you were away."

"That's a relief," Richard said.

"I hope the Brigade can call on you again," said Aric. He was guiding the cargo ship out of Threll's orbit and into space. "You have been wonderful."

"Thanks," said Richard. "Any time." He meant it.

"Ditto," said Henry.

"Good," said Aric. "And now are you ready?"

Richard and Henry knew what to do. They

stood up and closed their eyes. As they clasped each other's hands, Richard called, "Good-bye, Aric. I'll miss you."

But if Aric answered, Richard didn't hear him. First he was in deep space. And then he was home.

School started a few days later. Richard, who was wearing his Interspace Brigade T-shirt, looked around the classroom. George, he saw, wore a shirt with tropical flowers all over it. Jennifer wore a dolphin pin from Ocean World. And Leroy had on a brand-new Baseball Hall of Fame jacket. Finally Henry showed up. He was wearing an old sweatshirt.

"Hi," said Richard. He looked closely at his friend's face. "What's that pink mark on your cheek?" he asked. "And how come you're not wearing your Brigade T-shirt?"

"I *was* wearing it," said Henry. "Until this girl from the sixth grade ran up and kissed me. Ugh! So I took it off and put my sweatshirt on. I'm not ready to be irresistible to women!"

Mrs. Marshall came into the classroom and sat down at her desk. "Good morning, everyone," she said. "It's so nice to see you all again! What did all of you do on your vacations?"

"I went to Ocean World and played with a dolphin," said Jennifer.

"I went to the Baseball Hall of Fame and saw Babe Ruth's baseball bat," said Leroy.

"I went to this island called Tortola," said George.

"Is that in the Virgin Islands, George?" asked Mrs. Marshall.

"I'm not sure," said George. "But it sure was hot. My whole back is peeling from sunburn. Wanna see?"

"Don't be gross, George," said Celia Drummond. She was wearing a Minnie Mouse watch, Richard noticed. As he loooked at her, she smiled at him. She had hardly ever even noticed him before.

"And how about you, Henry?" asked Mrs. Marshall. "Did you do anything interesting?"

"Uh, not really," mumbled Henry, who was a terrible liar.

"Well, what *did* you do?" asked Mrs. Marshall.

Richard knew Henry needed help. He raised his hand.

"Yes, Richard?" As Mrs. Marshall called on him, her eyes fell on Richard's T-shirt for the first time. Suddenly her voice and expression changed. They both got very sweet, and a dazed look came into her eyes.

"Henry and I took a trip together," said Richard.

"How nice! I hope you had a good time." Mrs. Marshall was practically cooing at Richard.

"We did," said Richard. "We met a lot of interesting, uh, people. We ate some really . . . unusual food. And we helped out a friend.

That was the best part, right, Henry?"

Henry smiled at his friend. "Right," he said.

"Well, I think that's just about the nicest thing I've ever heard, Richard," said Mrs. Marshall with a huge smile. "Perhaps you'd like to do a special report on your vacation in front of the class . . . we could invite the principal!" She was beaming as though she had just given him a medal.

"Uh . . . thanks, but no, Mrs. Marshall, I—"

Just then the bell rang. Before it had stopped ringing Richard was out of the classroom. He raced to the bathroom and pulled off his Interspace Brigade T-shirt. Luckily he had a sweater in his backpack that he could wear instead.

"Boy, that was close," he said to Henry, who was waiting for him in the hallway. "You were right. Those T-shirts are dangerous!"

Henry smiled. "But we could wear them every now and then. Like when Mrs. Marshall is making out report cards."

"I always knew you were a genius," said Richard. And they walked down the hall to science class.

About the Authors

JONATHAN ETRA is a novelist and magazine journalist. He lives for dessert, but says, "It always takes at least 11,976 years to get here." Jonathan Etra lives in New York City.

STEPHANIE SPINNER is a children's book editor and author who lives in New York City. She never eats dessert.

About the Illustrator

STEVE BJÖRKMAN is an artist whose work often appears in advertisements, magazines, and greeting cards. He notes, "I have been drawing ever since I was a kid. I was often reprimanded for doodling in class and now find it a great relief to do a drawing without having to hide it from the teacher." Steve Björkman lives in Irvine, California.